The Four Fisherwomen

--- Recognizing the VALUE of our common GOOD ---

Copyright © 2014, The Mountain of Miracles

http://www.themountainofmiracles.com
Printed in the United States of America.

Published under The Mountain of Miracles
Written & Designed by Cleous G. Young

ISBN-13: 978-0692231012
Imprint: (The Mountain of Miracles)
ISBN-10: 0692231013

Cover Design by: Osrick Ingredients Cricket

The Four Fisherwomen (TFF) is a part of a S.E.T (<u>S</u>upportive <u>E</u>ducational

<u>T</u>ool) that acts as a supplemental teamwork with **Do Your Best** (DYB).

TFF focuses on **Horizontal** learning while DYB focuses on **Vertical**

learning. Together, they help the reader horizontally relate to others and

vertically grow independently. The S.E.T is a part of our **Literacy 4 Peace**

Campaign, which focuses on getting readers to **comprehend** more from

what they read. The more the reader comprehends, the more he or she

grasps. The more the person grasps, the more he or she will understand.

Through understanding, the person is able to gain knowledge.

Knowledge is Power. The use of Power causes an element to move/grow.

Special Thanks to the valuable inputs and reflections from our focus groups:

Women & Seniors:
Mrs. Emily Hill Rollins, Linda Whiteside, Anilda Davila, Paulena Thomas, Patricia Whitehead, Natasha Harris-Foster, Asttarte Jennifer Rose, Terena Clements, Kimberly Curette, Karen Joseph, and Judy Winter.

Men & Seniors:
Andrew Jackson, Wakeel Shabazz, Maurice Henderson, Michael Reid, Joseph Manning and Hasan Roland Sharpe.

Children:
Janiya Hicks, Gregory Bonaparte Jr., Bernard Hicks, Najee Francis, Joseph Manning III, Quasim Manning, Isreal Ortez, Kiera Braby, Kina Mitchell and Diamond Mitchell.

Special thanks to the support of my mother **Carol Nelson** and my father **Melvin Young.** Their parental roles have tremendously helped to open up the gateway of my confidence, my ability and my faith in the world. To this, I attest that the greatest support a child could ever have invested in their needs come from his or her parents.

Instructions:

1. Please take your time to read the story, fill in the drawings, and answer the questions. This interactive portion allows you to be **involved** in the story. The more you are involved in doing something, the more you will get out of that thing. See the Chinese proverb below.

2. Reread the story so you can get its full effect.
    1. Rereading the story more than once will give you a better understanding of the story.
        i. This is similar to practicing a game or sport; the more you **practice** the better you will become.
    2. Rereading the story more than once will also fill you in on what you missed the first time around.

3. Enjoy the story and have fun with it... Reading is FUNDamental... It **FUNDS** Your Mental, which en**rich**es your life, only when you comprehend what you read. The process of reading funds your mentality, and the process of comprehending what was read, enriches your life.

4. There are two sections to the book:
    1. The first section is the basic story, which is typically for the child only.
    2. The second section includes the author's view, which may require an adult **involvement**. This is an attempt to encourage adult involvement, which should increase different levels of the child. According to the National Education Association's website (www.nea.org), the report, a synthesis of research on parent involvement over the past decade,

also found that, regardless of family income or background, students with involved parents are more likely to:

- Earn higher grades and test scores, and enroll in higher-level programs.
- Be promoted, pass their classes, and earn credits.
- Attend school regularly.
- Have better social skills, show improved behavior, and adapt well to school.

*** **Chinese Proverb:** Tell me, I will forget. Show me, I will remember. **Involve me**, I will understand.

The Four Fisherwomen

--- Recognizing the VALUE of our common GOOD ---

Me: Hi! My name is Four Fisherwomen. Nice to meet you...What is your name?

You: My name is _____

Me: Thank you for choosing to read me today. Please enjoy. See you soon...

Once upon a time, there were four women of four different shades of color. Who lived with four different husbands. Who had four different thoughts. Who occupied four different ages. Who raised four different children, and if you are starting to see the pattern of many fours, well here comes more. They spoke four different languages, groomed in four different cultures, dressed in four different styles and in addition, resided in four different parts of the earth. You could call this rhythm of four, the fourth dimension. [**Q: What is the most common thing in this first paragraph?**]

*Hi, it's me again. Please use the provided box on the next page to draw your version of the four fisherwomen. Make it cool and draw yourself in the picture as well, which means that you will be right next to the Four Fisherwomen.

Though they were in four different parts of the earth, with four different husbands, four different shades of color, raised four different children, occupied four different ages, spoke four different languages, groomed in four different cultures, dressed in four different styles, and had four different thoughts, they all had one thing in common: a husband that loved to fish. Of these four fisherwomen, one lived in the N for North, E for East, W for West, and _____ for South. *If you guessed the letter "S," then you got it right*. And so it was, that these women only had one thing in common with each other, at least that is what it seemed like. [Q: **Name a sport that you are aware of that has four quarters in it?**]

* It's me again, FFW. Can you think of a navigation tool that uses these same four letters that were mentioned previously? Use the box to draw the tool and then label it afterwards with the letters.

Label it: _____

One day, each of the women decided to go fishing by themselves. *Well, well, well, what about that? They had their second thing in common, which was to go fishing by themselves.*

"Bob, I will catch a big one today so I can make you some fish soup. I am sure this soup will make you feel much,

much better and get you well again," said each wife to her husband. Oh my goodness! All four men were named Bob. That was the third thing that they all had in common. Yet, they were in four different parts of the earth. One lived in the N, the other in the E, the third was in the W, and the last one was in the _____. *If you guessed the letter S, you got that one right, again. Good job so far! Keep that greatness coming!*

Off the four fisherwomen went to the deep, deep ocean to catch one big fish, to make one good pot of soup and to get back to their one good husband. The four fisherwomen went to their separate docks. They hopped into four different boats and they carried four different fishing poles. However, they all went in one direction: to the deep, deep ocean. *Well, well, well; what do we have here? Another thing in common!* This was the fourth thing that they had in common, yet none of them knew about each other. [**Q: What would you take fishing if you were in this situation?**]

It's me again. Do you know the name of one of the five major oceans?

_____

And so it was, that after they began to travel at sea,

something transformed about them and none of them could

tell the difference. Their fishing poles, their boats, their colors,

and their clothing had all taken on the color of the ocean. I

mean literally... All four fisherwomen were on the same level

of oneness, where none of them were better than the other.

Yet, none of them noticed such major personal and

environmental changes. *Well, well, well; I think we have*

another one here! This was their fifth thing in common. Soon

they were all located in one steady location with their boats.

Well, well, well; the sixth thing in common. [Q: **Why do you**

think they had to remain still in their boats?]

It wasn't long before the four fisherwomen began to cast

their rods into the deep, deep ocean. *Well, well, well; what do*

we have here? Almost! This time around, they entered what

was called the Ping-Pong Fishing method. This was a

dynamic way of fishing. N casted her rod first, which allowed E

to cast her rod second. W was the next person to cast her rod.

Last but not least, was ___. *If you guessed the letter "S," you got it right. You are super-duper good at this! Keep up the confidence.*

And so it was, that all four fisherwomen entered the Ping-Pong Fishing method. One person had to cast their rod before the other person could cast theirs, which was similar to playing the game of Ping-Pong; one person had to serve the ball before the second person could knock the ball back over.

Soon, the first fish was caught: a BIG red one. Take a wild guess by whom? Drum roll please... The letter "S." Remember, it was called the Ping-Pong Fishing method. This meant that the first person down had to be the last person up, which meant it was the letter S's chance to play, according to the rules of the game of Ping-Pong. However, if S did not catch a fish, W, E and N would still be without a fish. That was how the dynamics of the Ping-Pong Fishing method worked. N had to serve the ball, which was casting the rod. In order for N to hit the ball again, S had to hit the ball back over. Therefore, S had to catch a fish before W. W would have to catch a fish before E. And E would catch a fish before ___ got a chance to catch hers. And this was the process of the Ping-Pong Fishing method. It was a sequence of ORDER, and there was no way around this method once **you** were in the deep, deep ocean.

[Q: Name four things that happened in the story so far?]

*It's me again. This time I want you to draw and color a big red fish in the box. Be creative and add some flavor to it. By the way, my favorite color is green. What is your favorite color? _____

Before you get back to the story, let us take a breather from it and have you do a fun exercise. Are you up for this challenge? Are you sure? All right, let's do it. This is a tongue twister, tongue twister, tongue twisterrrrrr. Ready? Say the following phrase as fast as you can: "Four Fisherwomen Fished For Four Big Fish to make Fish Soup For Four Fantastically Fickle-Minded Fathers."

- So, how did you do? Can you do it faster? Are you sure? Go!
- Challenge someone to do it. Do you think the person would do it better than you would? Try it and see. Remember to thank the person afterwards.
- Now, relax your tongue and let us get back to the story. Good job!

If their fishing did not take place in order, this meant that they could be out in the ocean all day trying to catch a big fish, as they had **promised** their husbands. This also meant that their husbands would still be sick. Depending on how sick they were, this could mean the difference between life and death. So all of the women's fishing hopes were in whether S caught a fish or not, yet none of them were aware of this powerful Ping-Pong Fishing method. *Now, do you understand the Ping-Pong Fishing method? Explain it to someone and see if you got it. If you did, give yourself a pat on the back. You have done a great job! If not, reread this section until you comprehend it and you are able to explain it. This is the most powerful lesson of this story.*

Of course, it wasn't long before four BIG red fish were caught. *Well, well, well, what do we have here? Another thing in common.* This was their seventh thing they had in common. The eighth thing they had in common was right around the corner. All four BIG red fish were the same size and weighed the same amount. *Well, well, well, what did we notice here?* The fish were all the same size and weight, despite being in four different locations. **Mmmm, I often wondered how that happened.** Nevertheless, the four fisherwomen were very happy with their BIG catch, as they had **promised** their husbands. For them, it was like a dream come true. [Q: **Name one thing that you promised you were going to do and did it.**]

On their way back to the docks, they returned to their normal color, clothing, boat, and rod. It was something mysterious that the deep, deep ocean did on its own and no one could ever explain it. It was like getting a small cut on your body, which then healed by itself. None of the four fisherwomen noticed any form of change as everything seemed normal to them. Therefore, they could not change what they did not notice. They were too focused on what was important, which was getting their husbands well. Thus, this was their ninth thing they had in common. *Well, well, well; even when it wasn't noticeable, they had something in common.* Soon, they were safely home. They cooked up a wonderful fish soup and fed their sickly husbands. It wasn't long before all four husbands were out of bed, feeling great and back to their normal life. A part of this great feeling was because their wives kept their promise of catching a BIG fish.

*Guess who? It's me, FFW. This time I want you to try to draw a small boat on the ocean. There is no right or wrong way to draw your boat on an ocean. Just take your time and do the best you can. To make it interesting, draw yourself in the boat fishing. You can do it! ☺

Since they had kept their promise, and cooked a wonderful fish soup, these two things became their tenth and eleventh things they had in common. *Well, well, well; what do we have here? Eleven things in common so far, yet we started out with just one. Oh, did you see one more thing they had in common? Yes, they all reached home safely. This was their twelfth thing they had in common. Did you notice this as well?*

If you did, you are paying attention! That's an A + for you and two pats on the back! You are doing a fantastic job!

Now that the husbands were out of bed and feeling great, they bought four nice leopard skin purses. They gave their beautiful wives four kisses on the cheek before handing them their special gift. All four couples lived happily ever after, all because the four fisherwomen kept their promise. *Well, well, well; what do we have here? Their sixteenth thing in common. Just in case you missed it, and I know the ones who are paying attention didn't based on their attention skill. The fourteenth thing they had in common was the leopard skin purse. Find the 13th, 15th things in common and also the 17th?*

Well, well, well. I must give it to you! *You did a fantabulous job! That's all folks!*

The End!

Well, well, well...Here comes the next portion of the book, which is to take what you have just read and apply it to your own life. The FFW would like to challenge you. Are you up for a challenge? Well, here goes...

FFW's Challenge:

Find someone that you don't know and locate things you have in common with that person, just as the story did. Explain the activity to the person before proceeding. And guess what? Though it is a challenge to you, it will bridge a beautiful reward of you discovering a new you and the true **value** of the other person. Yippie! I am really, really proud of you for taking on this challenge! Congratulations in advance for discovering a new you! You can use the **Commonality Test** in the back of the book as a guide to your activity. As always, DO YOUR BEST.

Questions:

1. *Do you think that any of your drawings may be the same as someone else that read the same story? _____*

   a. *What about your answers to the fill in the blank questions? _____*

2. *Do you know anyone that you can compare your drawings and answers with? _____*

3. *Did you personally have anything in common with the drawings or answers? _____*

4. *What do you think causes people to have things in common?*

   _____
   _____
   _____

5. *What was the four fisherwomen's promise to the husbands, and what was the worst thing that could happen if they broke their promise?*

   _____
   _____
   _____
   _____

6. *How does question number 5 personally relate to your life or an experience you had?*

_____

_____

_____

_____

7. *What was the common number in the story?*

_____

8. *Where did all four fisherwomen live?* _____ _____

_____ & _____

9. *How many fish were they supposed to catch and why?*

_____

_____

_____

10. *How many things did they have in common?*

_____

11. *What method did they encounter in the middle of the ocean?*

_____

_____

12. *What was the main thing that they had in common which they all depended on?*

_____

_____

_____

***You must come to the understanding that the universe that we reside in offers the opportunity for all of us to be connected as ONE: the SOUP. Whether it is human beings, plants, animals, fish, water, land, insects, etc., we are all connected. Science teaches us that we get our oxygen from plants and vitamin D from the sun. Therefore, though we are individually different, we are dependently connected. Two people can be in two different parts of the world and connect with each other through a telephone call. Before telephones, there was telepathy. Telepathy still exists in today's universe, and it still works effectively. This story's intent was to create a fictional look at the Universe through the eyes of the deep, deep ocean. The power of the story is seen in the fact that none of these women actually met each other, yet they all did the same thing and had many things in common. However, they got closer to each other all because of their sick husbands. This is the same for the reality of our life. We tend to come closer together when there is a disaster (husbands were sick), such as death in the family, 9-11, an earthquake, a flood, a school shooting, a tsunami, etc. This is when we tend to overlook the differences and bond with the common, which is the disaster.

Having things in common, known as commonality, is not just a figment of the mind. It is what bonds us together. It is the glue that keeps up together and alive. It is what we use to live our daily lives, even if we don't take note of it. For instance, language is a thing that we all have in common, and we use it every day to live among each other without being aware of it. Common is the strength of you, me and everything that dwells within the Universe. The more we use it, the more we become the Soup that heals everyone. For more information on this, you can check out the 101 Dalmatian Principle from the book E 2(Squared) by Pam Grout.

*We sometimes find it easy to harm someone or damage something around us, yet we never know how connected that person or thing is to us. When we destroy it, we are destroying the connection that it has with us. This is why the Ping-Pong Fishing method was the most powerful lesson of the story. You play Ping-Pong with everyone and everything around you. What common things do we share with that person or thing? What if they were the Ping-Pong Partner who had to return the ball for us to play? Mmmm, have you ever thought about that? Before you harm someone or something, please think about what part of **you** that you will be destroying!*

- **PS.** Just in case you haven't found the 17th element they had in common, it was their kept promise to their husbands.
- The five major oceans are (1. Pacific 2.Atlantic 3. Indian 4. Southern 5. Artic)

Answers:

- The first three questions are open-ended with a "Yes" or "No" answer.

- Question number 4 is open-ended, which is to have the reader think. One of the answers to that question is that we are all the creature of human beings and we belong to the same homosapien group.

- Question number 5 is also open-ended. However, this answer is provided from the text. They all promised their husbands that they would catch a big fish, come home and make a pot of fish soup and get them well again. The worst thing that could happen if they broke their promise was that the husbands might die.

- Question number 6 is also an open-ended question. However, this question draws from a personal experience. Answers may differ.

- The answer for question number 7 is the number 4.

- Question number 8 was taken directly from the text. They lived in the North, East, West & South.

- Question number 9 was also taken directly from the text. They were supposed to catch one big fish to make one good pot of soup to help their one good husband get well.

- Question number 10 was directly taken from the text as well. They had 17 things in common.

- Question number 11 was also taken from the text. They encountered the Ping-Pong Fishing method in the middle of the ocean.

- Question number 12 was also taken from the text. The main thing that they had in common was that they all depended on was also the Ping-Pong Fishing method.

The Four Fisherwomen

--- Recognizing the VALUE of our common GOOD ---

Me: Hi! My name is Four Fisherwomen. Nice to meet you...What is your name?

You: My name is _____

Me: Thank you for choosing to read me today. Please enjoy. See you soon...

Once upon a time, there were four women of four different shades of color. Who lived with four different husbands. Who had four different thoughts. Who occupied four different ages. Who raised four different children, and if you are starting to see the pattern of many fours, well here comes more. They spoke four different languages, groomed in four different cultures, dressed in four different styles and in addition, [resided] in four different parts of the earth. You could call this rhythm of four, the fourth [dimension].

Comment [nu1]: To live in a place permanently or for an extended period.

Comment [nu2]: The length, width, height, or depth of something

Though they were in four different parts of the earth, with four different husbands, four different shades of color, raised four different children, occupied four different ages, spoke four different languages, groomed in four different cultures, dressed in four different styles, and had four different thoughts, they all had one thing in common: a husband that loved to fish. Of these four fisherwomen, one lived in the N for North, E for East, W for West, and _____ for South. *If you guessed the letter "S," then you got it right.* And so it was, that these women only had one thing in [common] with each other, at least that is what it seemed like.

Comment [nu3]: Comment [nu4]: Belonging equally to, or shared alike by, two or more or all in question.

One day, each of the women decided to go fishing by themselves. *Well, well, well, what about that? They had their second thing in common, which was to go fishing by themselves.*

"Bob, I will catch a big one today so I can make you some fish soup. I am sure this soup will make you feel much, much better and get you well again," said each wife to her husband. Oh my goodness! All four men were named Bob. That was the third thing that they all had in common. Yet, they were in four different parts of the earth. One lived in the N, the other in the E, the third was in the W, and the last one was in

the _____. *If you guessed the letter S, you got that one right, again. Good*

job so far! Keep that greatness coming!

Off the four [**fisherwomen**] went to the deep, deep

ocean to catch one big fish, to make one good pot of soup and

to get back to their one good husband. The four fisherwomen

went to their separate docks. They hopped into four different

boats and they carried four different fishing poles. However,

they all went in one direction: to the deep, deep ocean. ***Well,***

well, well; what do we have here? Another thing in common!

This was the fourth thing that they had in common, yet none of

them knew about each other.

It's me again. Do you know the name of any of the five major oceans?

_____

And so it was, that after they began to travel at sea,

something   [**transformed**] about them and none of them

could tell the difference. Their fishing poles,

their boats, their colors, and their clothing [**had all taken on**

the color of the ocean.] I mean [**literally**]…All four fisherwomen were on the same level of oneness, where none of them were better than the other. Yet, none of them noticed such major personal and environmental changes. *Well, well, well; I think we have another one here! This was their fifth thing in common.* Soon they were all located in one steady location with their boats. *Well, well, well; the sixth thing in common.*

Comment [nu8]: To throw or move (something) in a forceful way.

It wasn't long before the four fisherwomen began to [cast] their rods into the deep, deep ocean. *Well, well, well; what do we have here? Almost!* This time around, they entered what was called the [Ping-Pong] Fishing method. This was a

Comment [nu9]: To move or transfer back and forth.

dynamic way of fishing. N casted her rod first, which allowed E to cast her rod second. W was the next person to cast her rod. Last but not least, was ___. *If you guessed the letter "S," you got it right. You are super-duper good at this! Keep up the confidence.*

And so it was, that all four fisherwomen entered the Ping-Pong Fishing method. One person had to cast their rod before the other person could cast theirs, which was similar to [playing the game of Ping-Pong]; one person had to serve

Comment [nu10]: Everything a person does affect someone else, locally or internationally.

the ball before the second person could knock the ball back over.

Soon, the first fish was caught: a BIG red one. Take a wild guess by whom? Drum roll please...The letter "S." Remember, it was called the Ping-Pong Fishing method. This meant that the first person down had to be the last person up, which meant it was the letter S's chance to play, according to the rules of the game of Ping-Pong. However, if S did not catch a fish, W, E and N would still be without a fish. That was how the dynamics of the Ping-Pong Fishing method worked. N had to serve the ball, which was casting the rod. In order for N to hit the ball again, S had to hit the ball back over. Therefore, S had to catch a fish before W. W would have to catch a fish before E. And E would catch a fish before ___ got a chance to catch hers. And this was the process of the Ping-Pong Fishing method. It was a sequence of [**ORDER**], and there was no way around this method once **you** were in the deep, deep ocean.

Comment [null]: The world operates with in an orderly method. Order is what helps to keep us aligned. Otherwise, we will be all over the place. Noticed that all the women were now in on one accord.

If their fishing did not take place in order, this meant that they could be out in the ocean all day trying to catch a big fish, as they had **promised** their husbands. This also meant that their husbands would still be sick. Depending on how sick they were, this could mean the difference between life and death. So all of the women's fishing hopes were in whether S caught a fish or not, **[yet none of them were aware]** of this powerful Ping-Pong Fishing method. *Now, do you understand the Ping-Pong Fishing method? [Explain it to someone] and see if you got it. If you did, give yourself a pat on the back. You have done a great job! If not, reread this section until you comprehend it and you are able to explain it. This is the most powerful lesson of the story.*

Comment [nu12]: Though we are independent to our own living, our life is depending on someone or something else. This is seen within the internal organs of the body; each organ is independent, but they all come together to operate the entire body. We are a living Organ, that works with other Organs to make a large body works; the Universe. Yet, not too many are not aware of their independent living and dependent process.

Comment [nu13]: Create an example in your life and see what you cannot do if there is something missing. Then reverse it. What cannot get done without you? Therefore, when you explain something to someone, you are depending on that person. Otherwise, your explanation just drifts off into space.

Of course, it wasn't long before [**four BIG red fish**] were caught. ***Well, well, well, what do we have here? Another thing in common.*** This was their seventh thing they had in common. The eighth thing they had in common was right around the corner. All four BIG red fish were the same size and weighed the same amount. ***Well, well, well, what did we notice here?*** The fish were all the same size and weight, despite being in four different locations. [**Mmmm, I often wondered how that happened**].

Nevertheless, the four fisherwomen were very happy with their BIG catch, as they [**had promised their husbands**]. For them, it was like a dream come true.

On their way back to the docks, they returned to their normal color, clothing, boat, and rod. It was something mysterious that the deep, deep ocean did on its own and no one could ever explain it. It was like getting a small cut on your body, which then healed by itself. None of the four fisherwomen noticed any form of change as everything seemed normal to them. Therefore, they could not change

what they did not notice. They [**were too focused**] on what

> Comment [nu17]: Focusing on something that is important will take away our focus on things that are not so important.

was important, which was getting their husbands well. Thus,

this was their ninth thing they had in common. *Well, well, well;*

even when it [wasn't noticeable], they had something in common.

> Comment [nu18]: What do you have in common with the person next to you that you never noticed before?

Soon, they were safely home. They cooked up a wonderful

fish [**soup**] and fed their sickly husbands. It wasn't long before

> Comment [nu19]: A liquid food made by boiling or simmering meat, fish, or vegetables with varies added ingredients.
>
> - Please note that we are the SOUP of the Earth; when we come together, we make something that is healthy for everyone.

all four husbands were out of bed, feeling great and back to

their normal life. A part of this great feeling was because their

wives kept their promise of catching a [**BIG**] fish.

> Comment [nu20]: We grow so much bigger when we see the common good in each other…

Since they had kept their promise, and cooked a

wonderful fish soup, these two things became their tenth and

eleventh things they had in common. *Well, well, well; what do we*

have here? Eleven things in common so far, yet we started out with

just one. Oh, did you see one more thing they had in common? Yes, they all reached home safely. This was their twelfth thing they had in

common. Did you notice this as well?

You are paying attention! That's an A + for you and two pats on the back! You are doing a fantastic job!

> **Comment [nu21]**: The universe is like a nice leopard skin; the dots resemble the nice people and things, which are all connected to the same nice skin (universe). Now, when one dot is affected, the entire skin feels it.

Now that the husbands were out of bed and feeling

great, they bought four [**nice leopard skin purses**]. They

gave their beautiful wives four kisses on the cheek before

[**handing them their special gift**]. All four couples lived

> **Comment [nu22]**: When people feel great about themselves, they become a special gift, which they will gladly share with others.

happily ever after, all because the four fisherwomen

kept their promise. *Well, well, well; what do we have here? Their*

sixteenth thing in common. Just in case you missed it, and I know

the ones who are paying attention didn't based on their attention

skill. The fourteenth thing they had in common was the leopard skin

purse. Find the 13th, 15th things in common and also the 17th?

Well, well, well. I must give it to you! *You did a fantabulous job! That's all folks!*
The End!

> **Comment [nu23]**: Did you notice that the closer they got to their goal, the more they had in common? The closer we come together the more we will see that we have the same things in common, which represent the Leopard Skin. Even when we are on four different parts of the Earth, we are still connected.

[Side Note]

***You must come to the understanding that the universe that we reside in offers the opportunity for all of us to be connected as ONE: the SOUP. Whether it is human beings, plants, animals, fish, water, land, insects, etc., we are all connected. Science teaches us that we get our oxygen from plants and vitamin D from the sun. Therefore, though we are individually different, we are dependently connected. Two people can be in two different parts of the world and connect with each other through a telephone call. Before telephones, there was [telepathy].

Comment [nu24]: Something produced by the imagination.

Telepathy still exists in today's universe, and it still works effectively. This story's intent was to create a fictional look at the Universe through the eyes of the deep, deep ocean. The power of the story is seen in the fact that none of these women actually met each other, yet they all did the same thing and had many things in common. However, they got closer to each other all because of their sick husbands. This is the same for the reality of our life. We tend to come closer together when there is a disaster (husbands were sick), such as death in the family, 9-11, an earthquake, a flood, a school shooting, a tsunami, etc. This is when we tend to overlook the differences and bond with the common, which is the disaster.

Having things in common, known as commonality, is not just a [figment] of the mind. It is what bonds us together.

Comment [nu25]: A way of communicating thoughts directly from one person's mind to another person's mind without using words.

It is the glue that keeps up together and alive. It is what we use to live our daily lives, even if we don't take note of it. For instance, language is a thing that we all have in common, and we use it every day to live among each other without being aware of it. Common is the strength of you, me and everything that dwells within the Universe. The more we use it, the more we become the Soup that heals everyone. For more information on this, you can check out the 101 Dalmatian Principle from the book E 2 (Squared) by Pam Grout.

We sometimes find it easy to harm someone or damage something around us, yet we never know how connected that person or thing is to us. When we destroy it, we are destroying the connection that it has with us. This is why the Ping-Pong Fishing method was the most powerful lesson of the story. You play Ping-Pong with everyone and everything around you. What common things do we share with that person or thing? What if they were the Ping-Pong Partner who had to return the ball for us to play? Mmmm, have you ever thought about that? Before you harm someone or something, please think about what part of **you** that you will be destroying!

Write your <u>Reflection</u> of the things you became aware of just by reading this story: Feel free to share them with others, just as we have shared our knowledge with you in this story.

Commonality Test- The IRC

Name: _____

Objective: Your objective is to identify at least one favorite with another person and then create an activity around the thing that was identified. Just identify one common thing and see what will happen.

Identify: (You): Please use this section to identify your favorites. You can add other favorites by writing them down on a clean sheet of paper. The activity requires two or more people. For a large group, have each person rotate starting with # 1 and ending with # 10. For example, if one person's favourite color is blue, then all the other persons with blue as their favourite color would be grouped. Once all the favorite colors are grouped, then allow each person to observe with whom they have the same color in common. The observation is to show how our commonality joins us together, while our outer appearance may separate us. Next, do the same for favorite fruit. The groups from the colors will split up to form new groups of favorite fruits. You will repeat step one until you arrive at # 10, in which you will use this last favorite to do the activity section. Please, do your best and have fun, as you discover the **power** of having something in common with others.

1. What is your favorite **Color**? _____	2. What is your favorite **Fruit**? _____
3. What is your favorite **Meal** of the day?_____	4. What is your favorite **Season** of the year?_____
5. What is your favorite **Subject/Class**? _____	6. What is your favorite **Pet**? _____
7. Who is your favorite cartoon **Super Hero**? _____	8. What is your favorite day of the **Week**? _____
9. What is your favorite Movie?_____	10. What is your favorite **Sport**? _____

Relate: (Others): Please use this section to group the common people together.

1. What do you have in common

   _____

2. With whom do you have something in common?

   _____

Create: (Together): Please use this section to set a **foundation** of what you can create together.

1. What activity can you do together with your common thing/s?

   _____

   Example: You may go shopping for your favorite fruit or share tips about helping your pet.

2. Do you **promise** to create an activity per your provided answer to question # 1? YES __ or NO __

3. Do you think you will find more things in common as you do the activity?   YES__ or NO __

4. Please write down something important that you learned from doing the overall activity?

   _____

   _____

   _____

www.ingramcontent.com/pod-product-compliance
Lightning Source LLC
Chambersburg PA
CBHW081216170626
46811CB00010B/3314

9780692231012